THE MAGIC BOOTS

Story by SCOTT EMERSON and HOWARD POST

Illustrated by HOWARD POST

GIBBS·SMITH P PUBLISHER

SALT LAKE CITY

97 96   10 9 8 7 6 5

This is a Peregrine Smith Book, published by
Gibbs Smith, Publisher
P.O. Box 667
Layton, Utah 84041

Book design by Traci O'Very Covey

Printed and bound in Hong Kong

Library of Congress Cataloging-in-Publication Data

Emerson, Scott, 1959-

   The magic boots / story by Scott Emerson and Howard Post; illustrated by Howard Post.
        p. cm.

   Summary: William has a pair of magic cowboy boots that take him wherever he wants to go, but when he outgrows them, he makes a surprising discovery.

   ISBN 0-87905-603-7

   [1. Boots—Fiction. 2. Imagination—Fiction.] I. Post, Howard, 1948-   ill. II. Title.
PZ7.E5857Mag 1994   94-4036
[E]—dc20   CIP
                                               AC

DEDICATED

to the magic of childhood

Every morning when William Wilkins got out of bed, he brushed his teeth, patted his dog, Bob, and put on his cowboy boots.

They weren't just ordinary boots. For one thing, they were bright red. They were soft, too, as soft as Bob's ears.

But the most unordinary thing about William's cowboy boots was this: they were magic.

They weren't magic in the usual way. They didn't glow or throw off sparks or walk around by themselves. A miniature genie didn't live inside them. But when William put them on, he could go anywhere he wanted.

All he had to do was think of a place, anyplace, and in the blink of an eye he was there.

Just like that.

nce, he went canoeing down the Amazon River.

One time,
he spent the day
with Buffalo Bill's
Wild West Show.

And since he had always wanted to be a cowboy, at least once a week he took a herd of longhorns up the Chisholm Trail.

With the help of
the magic boots, William
travelled the world . . .
and he soon discovered that
all he had to do was hold
real tight, and Bob could
travel right along with him.

He made new friends,

and he learned to see things
from a different point of view.

But then, one day, it happened.
The most horrible, dreadful, ghastly, rotten,
worst thing William could imagine:
his feet would not fit inside the boots.

He took his socks off and sprinkled baby
powder on his feet. It didn't help.

He soaked his feet in ice water, hoping they
would shrink. They didn't.

inally, he faced the awful truth. His feet were just too big. He had outgrown the magic boots. All day long, he moped around, feeling sorry for himself, wishing he didn't have to grow up.

His mother tried everything to make him feel better. She even took him to get a new pair of high-tops.

It didn't help.

William couldn't get used to the idea that he would never again explore the Amazon, walk on the moon, or visit the Wild West.

That night, he cried himself to sleep, thinking about all the places he would never see again.

And suddenly,

he was back on the Chisholm Trail . . .

saving the Princess from the Black Knight . . .

and hang gliding over the Grand Canyon.

B

ut when he looked down, expecting to see the magic boots, all he saw were his own bare feet.

And at that moment, he realized it wasn't the boots that were magic.

It was him.

In the morning,
he bounded out of bed,
brushed his teeth until
they sparkled, gave Bob
a big hug, and put on
his new high-tops.

Then, as William stepped
out the back door,
he thought of a place
far away . . .

and in the blink of
an eye, he was there.